MW00902291

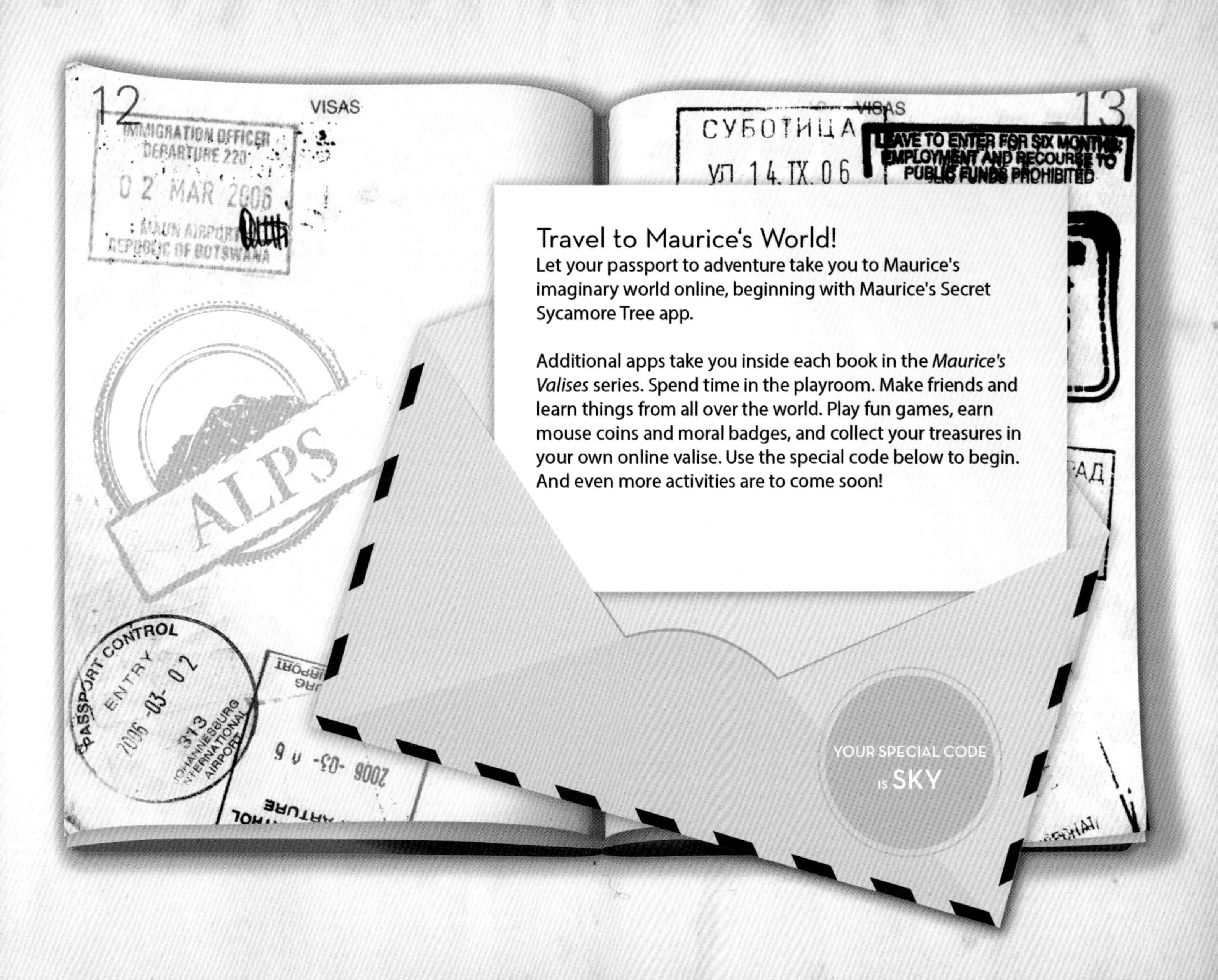

Travel to Maurice‘s World!
Let your passport to adventure take you to Maurice's imaginary world online, beginning with Maurice's Secret Sycamore Tree app.
Additional apps take you inside each book in the *Maurice's Valises* series. Spend time in the playroom. Make friends and learn things from all over the world. Play fun games, earn mouse coins and moral badges, and collect your treasures in your own online valise. Use the special code below to begin. And even more activities are to come soon!
YOUR SPECIAL CODE
IS SKY

The Books Before...

In the Beginning
In the first book, Maurice, an orphan mouse, travels to New Zealand, where he is visited by the Muse of Mice and is given a great responsibility. Maurice learns the value of always telling the truth.

The Micetro of Moscow
In the second book, Maurice travels to Russia, where he befriends a musical (yet unpopular) mouse, Henry, who helps Tchaikovsky finish *Swan Lake*. Maurice learns that everyone is special in his or her own way.

The Books Before...

Casablanca
In the third book, Maurice's adventures take him to Morocco, where a selfless act helps a bespectacled camel, Cecil, and Maurice learns the true meaning of friendship.

Medicine Mouse
In the fourth book, Maurice journeys to America. Traveling West, he befriends a kindly prairie dog, Pip, and meets a wise Medicine Mouse who shares his life's wisdom with Maurice.

A-B
C-D
E-F
G-H
I-J
K-L
M-N
O-P
Q-R
S-T
U-W

Do not believe in anything simply because it is found written in your religious books. Do not believe in anything merely on the authority of your teachers and elders. Do not believe in traditions because they have been handed down for many generations. But after observation and analysis, when you find that anything agrees with reason and is conducive to the good and benefit of one and all, then accept it and live up to it.

—*Buddha*

Everything we hear is an opinion, not a fact. Everything we see is a perspective, not the truth.

—*Marcus Aurelius*

Foreword

Letter to a Young Seeker: Journeying with Maurice and His Peaces (Moral Munchies)
—by Lama Surya Das

I was young, like you.

Like Maurice, I was a true seeker, but seekers can and eventually must become finders. Now Maurice and I are working to help restore balance and harmony in the world, knowing that the greatest journey is from head to heart.

Wisdom is easy to carry but difficult to gather. Some are wise and some are otherwise. Maurice has learned a great deal from both. When I was living in Nepal, in the Kathmandu Valley in sight of the year-round glistening snow peaks, my language teacher shared an old Nepali saying: that a good speaker needs no other tools. Maurice seems to be a part of that venerable lineage.

What we seek, we are. Travel broadens the mind and opens the heart, and pilgrimages nurture and nourish the soul. I had to go far out (and also abroad) in search of IT, only to find out that I am all that. And you are too!

Maurice often likes to remind us of this. A sign at the gate of a monastery I visited in Sri Lanka read: "Here you will find the atmosphere you have in mind." There I learned to turn my searchlight inwards; to be curious, patient, and resilient; to question my elders and their beliefs; and to discover my life values. And I learned to truly learn, to apply what I learned until it became part of me. You certainly can too—just like our good friend Maurice. Then every day will be a good day, and all the world will be a friend. There is no "way" to peace and happiness; peace and happiness are the way—we can walk it every day, in every moment. All is not exactly as it seems.

Keep your eyes peeled, your heart and mind open, attentive, alert, caring, curious, and aware. This book, the series, is full of meaningful delight. Like small but chock-full-o'-soul valises, you too can discover and uncover your story—your True Self—not someone's else's cookie-cutter-shaped model of what you "should" be. Wear the life that truly fits you; don't squeeze into someone else's. Pay attention! Wake up! As Maurice might say, if you're not here now, you won't be there to enjoy it. (He likes to say things like that, passing on the timeless wisdom he's gathered in his journeys.)

All aboard! Join the fun—deep fun, not just cheap thrills—that I have found right here. Help yourself!

Penned on the banks of the Mystic River, Massachusetts
May 2014

www.mauricesvalises.com

ISBN: 978-90-818368-3-8-51695

MOUSE PRINTS PRESS

Prinsengracht 1053-S Boot
1017 JE Amsterdam Netherlands

Maurice's Valises

Moral Tails in an Immoral World

Foreword by Lama Surya Das

Kookoo Mountain

By J. S. Friedman
Illustrations by Chris Beatrice

"Where's Kookoo Mountain, Grandpa?" asked Grindle, grandmouse number 91, the youngest of the lot.

He was leaning, gazing, where he always leaned and gazed—on the footstool of Grandpa Maurice's lumpy, bumpy storytelling chair.

"Well," said Maurice, rumpling the fur on Grindle's head, "Kookoo Mountain is up here." He pointed to his own head.

"And up here," Maurice continued, pointing to a tall stack of valises.

"And . . . it's also up in the Alps, tucked among the higher peaks.

"I call the mountain Kookoo because something really nutty happened up there.

"I'll tell you all about it as soon as the rest of your cousins arrive."

And so Grindle, who'd just learned to tell time, began to watch the wall clock.

PAW NOTE

A mountain-range system in Europe.

Three minutes and 11 seconds later, the front door burst open, and in rolled a few dozen merry mice and their friends, followed by a skipping trail of fallen leaves.

No one was dozy,
their cheeks were rosy,
the house was cozy,
and their autumn fur shined with twinkly frost.

And their giggles were many—but not for long. Once they realized that they were very late, a hush blanketed the room.

Everyone else was already seated, waiting for them in Maurice's living room, in the base of an old sycamore tree, deep in the woods.

As the latecomers warmed themselves by the fireplace, away from the gusty winds and autumn chills, Grandpa Maurice wasted no time.

"Call me Maurice," he said to his grandmice and their forest friends. Then he gazed up at his ceiling-high stack of dusty suitcases.

He carefully removed the valise marked "Kookoo Mountain," took it to his storytelling chair, and sat.

He jiggled the valise's latch and … and … it opened one-two-three.

Maurice chuckled to himself as he reached in and pulled out one pair of lederhosen, one white feather, one very large acorn, and, of course, one Moral Scroll.

Everyone was quiet as Maurice squeezed into the lederhosen. They were a bit snug—Maurice had eaten too many seeds over the years—but he could still sit, so he sat.

PAW NOTES

A paper with a wise saying written on it. The saying is the lesson learned from a particular traveling tale.

Strange leather shorts with suspenders, often worn by German-speaking mountain people.

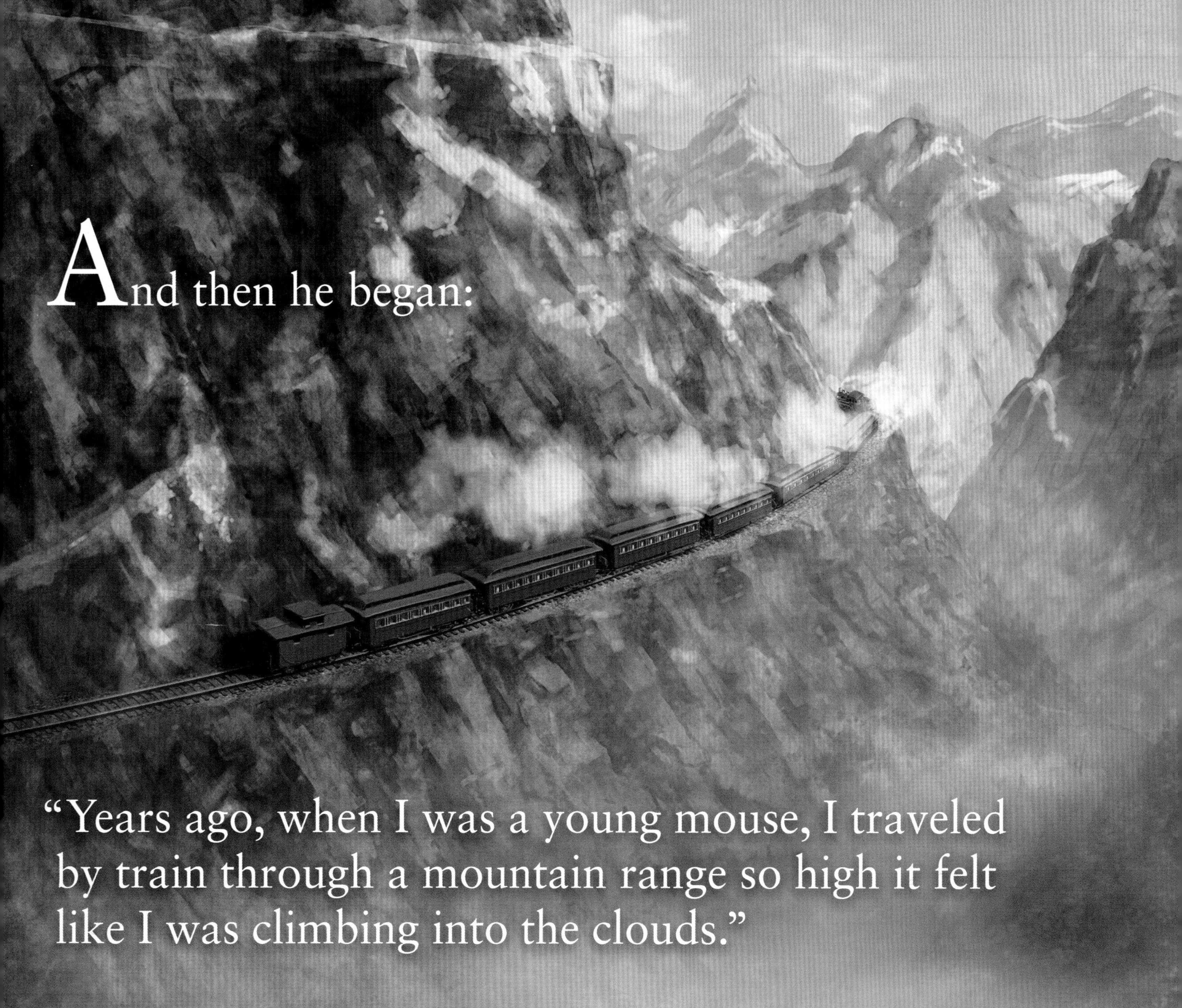

And then he began:

"Years ago, when I was a young mouse, I traveled by train through a mountain range so high it felt like I was climbing into the clouds."

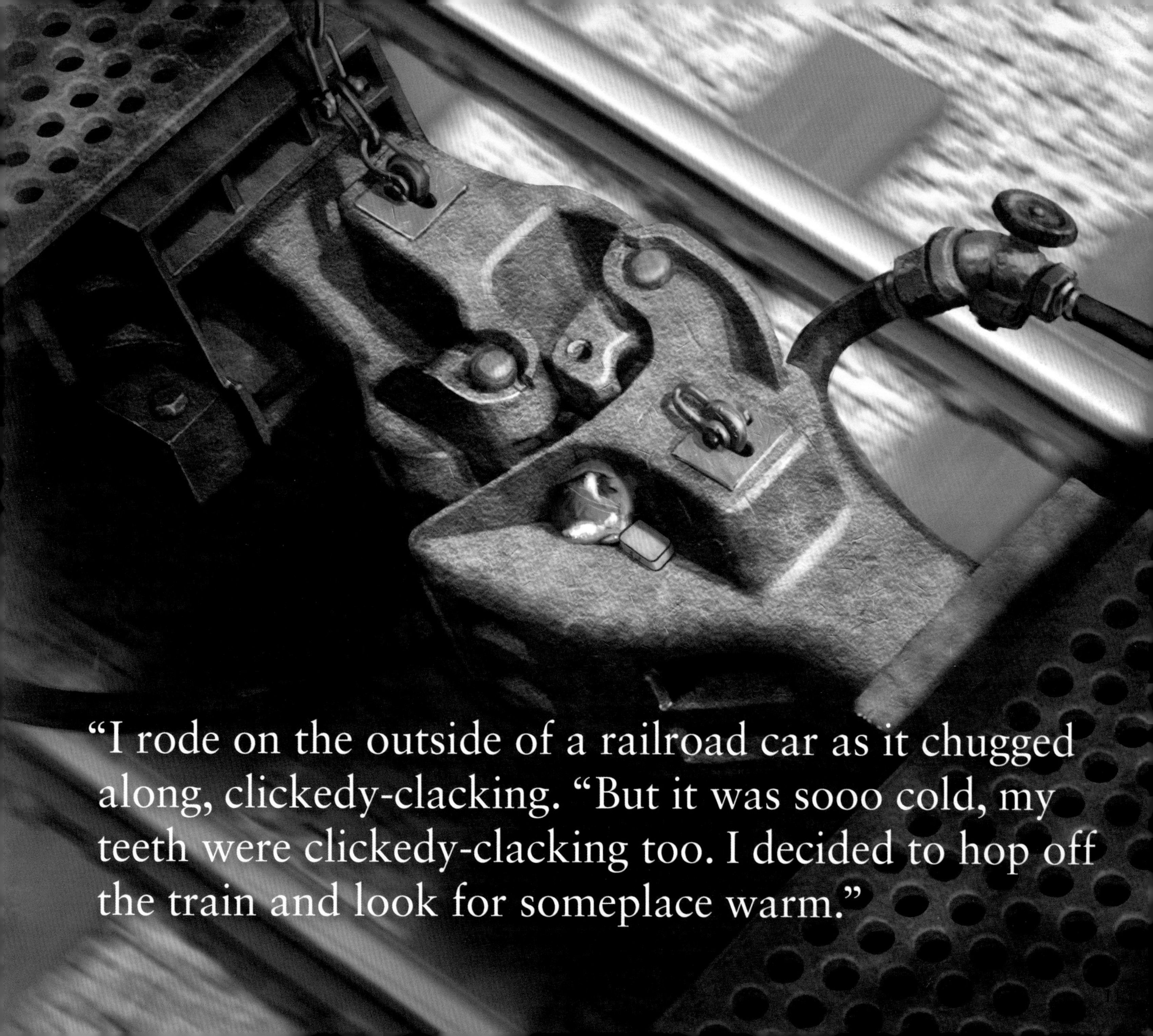

“I rode on the outside of a railroad car as it chugged along, clickedy-clacking. “But it was sooo cold, my teeth were clickedy-clacking too. I decided to hop off the train and look for someplace warm.”

"Soon the train began a slow descent into a small valley, where a station was nestled between the peaks.

"There the sun shone brightly, and there wasn't a bit of snow. And guess what? It was warm.

"So as the train crawled into the station, I threw my valise—and myself—onto the platform."

"Suddenly I heard a commotion.

"A crowd of men and boys—all in lederhosen, the local fashion—began rushing in all directions, carrying bundles and baskets of food.

"At first, I thought they were trying to catch the train. But soon a valley mouse poked his fuzzy brown head through a hole in the platform and yodeled me a warning:

"'Hey you, take cover!'"

PAW NOTE

Yodeling: a sing-songy calling out, made by alternating high-pitched sounds and falsetto, often done by cheese-loving mountain people.

"'Take cover? I am covered,' I replied.

"'Haven't you heard?' he scolded. 'The sky is falling!'

"'The sky, up there? That sky? Who said?' I asked.

"'Why, the prince, son of the late king. A piece of sky fell on his head today,' said the station mouse. 'He has made a proclamation to the whole valley.'"

“I had never, never, ever heard such a thing before—and I had already traveled far and wide, for being so young a mouse.

“Leaving the station seemed like a good idea, so I headed toward the nearby town.

“On the way, I met a squirrel—in lederhosen.

“He was hauling a sack of food, and his cheeks were stuffed with nuts.

“‘What is this about the sky falling?’ I asked.

“‘Sfave fyourfelf,’ is what I think he mumbled—it was hard to tell, because of all the nuts he spit as he talked.”

"Eventually, he spit out all the nuts, and I was able to piece together that earlier, as the prince sat outside on his throne in the castle courtyard, he was hit on the head by a piece of sky.

"Since the prince was alone at the time, Lord Vice Prince Chicanery, chief adviser to the prince, determined that the sky had fallen on the prince's head."

“So the prince and the lord vice prince decided to declare a state of emergency, which read:

“‘My fellow countrymen, we are in grave danger from above.

‘We must take care below.’

“‘Then,’ the squirrel continued, ‘the prince warned his advisers . . .

“‘who warned the townspeople . . .”

“‘who warned the farmers, who warned their farmhands.

“‘It wasn’t long before all the farm animals overheard.

“‘Even Oswyn, the snowy owl, heard. Everyone was in a state of panic.’

“‘Everyone?’ I asked the squirrel.”

"'Except Oswyn,' said the squirrel. 'Oswyn the owl didn't believe what he had heard.

"'Whoo, whoo,' said the owl.

"'Whooo is going to listen to such fwhooolishnesss?'

"Apparently," Maurice explained to his guests, "nobody listened to Oswyn the owl.

"Even though owls are known to be wise.

"Even though Oswyn knew a lot about the sky, since he spent so much time up there."

"Even though the owl hooted some pretty good questions, like:

"'Whooo can prove the sky is falling?

"'Whooo is to say this isn't a fantasy?

"'Whooo runs this kingdom?'

"Amazingly," chuckled Maurice, shaking his head as he remembered, "that squirrel didn't give a hoot what Oswyn said.

"The squirrel thought everyone should believe the prince, just because he was the son of the former king. And because you should always trust your rulers.

"The squirrel told me that everyone was supposed to bring baskets of food to the town square, for safe storage in the prince's counting house."

PAW NOTE

A place where money or other valuables is counted and stored.

"After dropping off the food, everyone was to return home until the prince solved the problem of the falling sky.

"I followed the squirrel to the town square, where we joined other animals, townspeople, and farmers.

"Everyone talked about the falling sky, though when I asked, no one had seen it fall.

"I kept looking for any sign that a piece of cloud or a slice of blue sky might be falling down."

“But when I looked up, all I saw was Oswyn the owl circling above, slowly flapping his wings.

“And when I looked down, all I saw were large stacks of food and bags of grain (and *flour*) in the town square.”

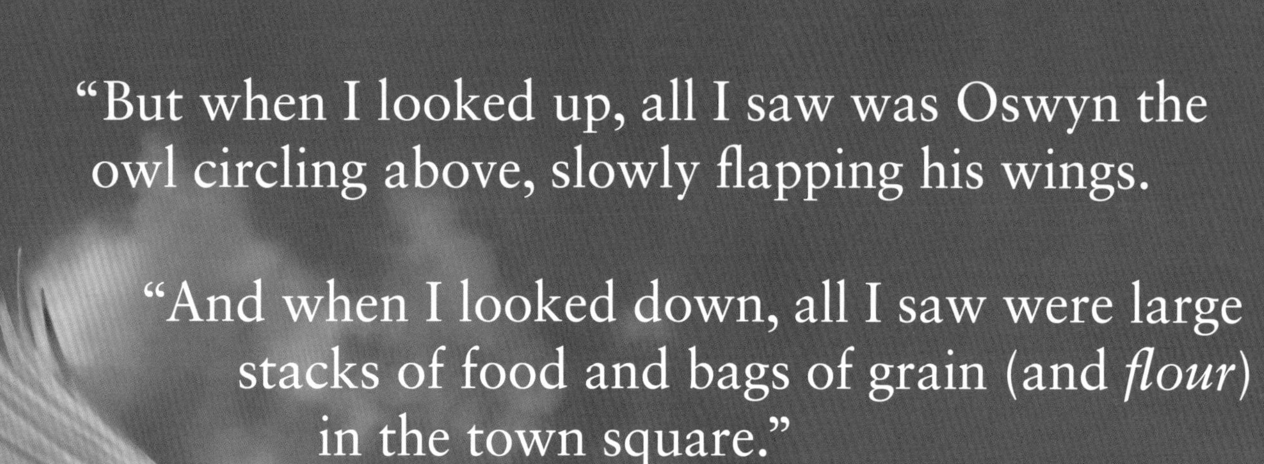

"And when I looked over, all I saw was the prince sitting on his throne, looking concerned.

"He ordered his guards to move the food into the castle.

"Then he ordered everyone else back to their homes.

"The castle mascot—the royal parrot, Fibber—squawked and squawked from his perch, 'The sky is falling, squawk, take cover.'

"He sounded exactly like the prince."

"High above the castle, Oswyn the owl could see the lord vice prince guiding the food from the town square to the back of the castle.

"There, without the king's subjects' knowledge, the food was divided among the prince's closest advisers' personal carts, for their own personal use.

"Oswyn the owl realized what was going on.

"And he was angry. Very, very, very angry."

"He flapped his wings so fast that feathers fluttered from the sky.

"Then he dropped something on the head of the prince.

"'The sky is falling again!' yelled the prince. 'Just like the lord vice prince said. It has been confirmed.'

"Then the prince dashed from his throne to the castle."

"Fibber the parrot squawked and parroted, 'Confirmed, confirmed, sky is falling, just like the lord vice prince said,' and then he flew to the safety of his castle cage.

"But this time … this time, everyone saw what had happened: Oswyn the wise owl had pooped on the prince's head!

"And that made them wonder, 'What had really fallen on the prince's head the first time around?'

"Curious, everyone went over to check the prince's abandoned throne under the giant oak tree."

“And there, on the ground around the throne, lay a blanket of acorns.

“It didn’t take long to figure out what had originally happened.

“The sky had not fallen on the prince’s head.

“An acorn had!

“Wiser, everyone returned to the town square and took back what was left of their bundles and bags of precious food.

“Then they returned to their homes.

“And they left the poor, befuddled prince, to whom they no longer listened, to deal with his own befuddlement.

“The end.”

There was a forest hush. There was not a sound in the room except for the hiss from the hearth.

“That’s why I call what happened ‘Kookoo,’” said Maurice, breaking the silence of the room.

“I would’ve asked questions like Oswyn,” exclaimed Grindle, “or at least I would’ve come up with some of my own.”

Maurice raised his eyebrows in merriment and said, “Let’s see what the Moral Scroll has to say.”

He unrolled the old paper full of holes.

He turned it, so all could see what was written.

And then he read:

Don't believe
all you hear.

Grindle, pleased with himself, looked around the room to see who was looking back.

Then he turned to look at Maurice.

There sat Maurice in his snug-fitting lederhosen, his eyes closed, already snoring: “Whooo . . . whooo . . .whooo . . . ,” like Oswyn..

“Who?” is a very important question—it’s right up there with “Where?” “What?” “When?” and, of course, “Why?”

Don’t forget to question.

The end, again
(But more to come . . .)

Don't Forget to Question . . .

We ask questions to better understand and to better trust what we hear. Should we ask each other some questions about this story?

What did the prince believe happened to him? Who tricked him into believing this? Should the prince have asked more questions?

Why did the prince's people believe the sky was falling? Should the people have also asked more questions?

Someone needs to be in charge—in a home, in a classroom, in a state, and in a country. Is it okay to ask questions of the person in charge?

The Moral Scroll says, "Don't believe all you hear." Is it telling you not to trust anyone? Whom do you trust?

The United Nations

The best leaders allow their people to ask them questions, give them ideas, and make them accountable. Being "accountable" means explaining why you did something and being responsible for all that happened because of what you did.

The leaders of countries are not only accountable to their people but to the entire world. A group of 193 countries or nations come together as the United Nations (or U.N.). The nations of the U.N. make sure that all member nations take responsibility for their actions. They strive to do these things:

Keep peace throughout the world.
Develop friendly relations between nations.
Work together to help people live better lives; eliminate poverty, disease, and illiteracy in the world; stop environmental destruction; and encourage respect for each other's rights and freedoms.
Be a center for helping nations achieve these aims.

Do you think it is easy for 193 nations to agree or to make change? No, it is not. But every day, thousands of people walk through the front doors of the U.N. to question, argue, agree, compromise, and try to make this a better world for all of us.

If you could go to the U.N. and talk to leaders from around the world, what would you tell them? What would you ask them? Would you hold them accountable? Would you tell them not to believe everything they hear?

It is not a crazy idea! Children have spoken to the U.N. many times. Malala Yousafzai, age 16, asked the U.N. to make sure all children are allowed to go to school. Severn Cullis-Suzuki, age 12, asked the nations to take better care of our planet. Everyone who asks questions can make a difference!

Explore more about the United Nations at your library or online at: www.un.org/cyberschoolbus/

Backwords

The Buddha was born as a prince named Siddhartha Gautama in Nepal almost 2,600 years ago. He was a wise human teacher who became Enlightened, opening his heart and mind to understanding life in the deepest way possible. The word "Buddha" is a title, meaning "one who is awake"—in the sense of having "woken up to reality" or "awakened from the sleep of illusion and confusion."

He said anyone—male, female, or other—could become Enlightened too, by practicing his famous Eightfold Path of Awakening.

Marcus Aurelius was a Roman emperor who was also known for being a Stoic philosopher. His reign and writings reflected his personal idea that to preserve equanimity in the midst of conflict, one follows nature as a source of guidance and inspiration.

Lama Surya Das (Jeffrey Miller) is a Buddhist leader, meditation teacher, chant-master, and poet. He is the author of over 13 books, including the international bestseller *Awakening the Buddha Within: Tibetan Wisdom for the Western World, Eight Steps to Enlightenment*, which has been translated into 13 languages. A columnist for The Huffington Post, Beliefnet, and other journals, he is the head of the Western Buddhist Teachers Network. Surya Das is affectionately called "The American Lama" by the Dalai Lama of Tibet.

Acknowledgments

The list of helpers I wish to acknowledge keeps growing as this series grows. To create the *Maurice's Valises* series and this book, *Kookoo Mountain*, I have repeatedly depended upon a brain trust of creative people.

My thanks to Fancy Pants Global of Iceland, and my special thanks to Elías R. Ragnarsson in Reykjavik for his diligence and humor in working at any hour of the day or night in the land of the midnight sun. To Stephanie Arnold for her editorial contributions from the very beginning. To Joe Landry for his supportive comments and typographic taste. To Kirsten Cappy for her insight and steerage in managing the children's-book world for me. To Renee Rooks Cooley for her copy-edit expertise, and to Marion of Colorset in Amsterdam for pre-pressing the pictures superbly. To my wife, Cheryl, thank you for tolerating and accepting Maurice as a new, ever-present family member.

And, as always, my many thanks to Chris Beatrice, whose inspired and magnificent illustrations have made my words come to life.